We're Moving Where?!

Glen Blackwell

Cover illustration by Sasha Brazhnik

Zoetrope Books

Published by Zoetrope Books 2020
Suffolk, England

A CIP catalogue record for this book is available from the
British Library

ISBN : 978-1-8383252-0-6

www.zoetropebooks.com

For Emily, Lucy and Sophie

Thank you for the inspiration and editorial
assistance!

Contents

Chapter 1

"Harry, can you come here for a minute, please?", called Jess.

"Yes Mum", groaned Harry. He was watching his favourite cartoon – Dinosaur Adventures – on TV and really didn't want to move.

"Come on Harry, we've got something exciting to tell you", Jess called again.

Harry swung his feet onto the floor and walked slowly backwards out of the room, eyes glued to the TV show all the way. He glanced sideways at his mum and dad, who were sitting at the kitchen table with a pile of magazines and a big notepad.

"Harry – we have some really great news", said his dad, with a big grin on his face. Mark Jones was a tall, softly spoken man with dark hair and his eyes sparkled with excitement as he spoke.

Harry finally drew his eyes away from the TV and walked over to the kitchen table. "What's up?", he said, with a faintly interested expression. He didn't really like having his TV time disturbed but something seemed worth listening to.

Jess slid the top magazine from the pile over to Harry – it was open on a double page spread showing a log cabin in the middle of a forest. "Harry – Dad's been offered a new job and we're going to move to Canada to live in a cabin like this", she said with a slightly nervous smile.

"Canada, where's that?", mumbled Harry, but inside he was thinking frantically. 'What about school and my friends?' 'Is it warm or cold?' 'Do they even have TV?!'

Mark moved the magazine on a few pages to reveal a map, "Canada is over the ocean, just here", he pointed with his finger. "It's about 6 hours on a plane."

Harry was thinking fast now and starting to worry a little. "Why do we have to go and do they have TV?", he said quickly, his voice rising as he spoke. "How will I get to school and to see my friends?"

"It's ok Harry", Jess moved over to put an arm around his shoulders. "Dad has been offered a great opportunity to study the animals living in the mountains of Canada. It means living right out in the wild and it'll be a great adventure."

"We'll be living in a tent to start with", added Mark, "then we'll build our own cabin where I can work too." He flipped back a page in the magazine to show the inside of a cosy looking log cabin. "This is what it will look like – all made of wood with proper rooms and everything."

"Yes", said Jess, "there won't be much that's normal compared with life now but it will be great for us to spend more time together and explore the great outdoors. We'll start off with school work from your old school which they're going to give us before we go and then we'll sign up for online classes from a school in Canada later."

Harry gathered up a pile of the magazines and took them back into the living room. There were some really interesting pictures – big mountains, blue lakes and lots and lots of trees. In one picture, a brown bear was fishing in a river, catching fish with his paw. 'Cool', thought Harry, 'I wonder if we'll have bears living next to us in Canada?'

Jess and Mark peered round the living room door, smiling at one another as they saw Harry looking through the magazines. It was good to see him showing an interest and apparently happy with the idea of their adventure.

"Mum?", Harry said as he looked up and saw them in the doorway, "where will our cabin be?" He pointed to the open magazine page – "There aren't any cabins in any of these pictures."

"We're being given a piece of land", Jess explained, "Dad's job will need him to be right in the forest so we'll be building a cabin in the woods. We can live there and he can study the animals at the same time."

"But where will we get the things to build it with?", persisted Harry, "wood and paint and stuff?" He could imagine it would be like building a den in the garden, although bigger. They had always gone to the shops to get things to help with den building and there weren't any shops in the pictures he'd been looking at.

"When we arrive, we'll be given some crates of materials", said Mark, "tools for building, some wood to build a frame and instructions on the best way to cut down trees for more wood."

"Epic!", shouted Harry, jumping to his feet in excitement, "so we'll be cutting down trees ourselves to build the cabin?" He made a chainsaw noise and danced around the room pretending to cut down trees, one after another.

"Steady", laughed Mark, "we'll have to be very careful when we do it to make sure they land in the right place and don't damage anything. It's also really important that we only take what we need from the forest and don't waste anything."

Harry thought for a moment and then spoke again – "When are we actually going?" It had seemed like just an exciting idea at first but the more his mum and dad talked about it, the more Harry realised they must have been planning it for a while.

Jess and Mark looked at each other. "We leave in 2 weeks, Harry", they said together.

"My new job is ready and waiting for me", Mark explained. "They want me to start as soon as I can – their government has allocated more money for animal research and they're keen to get someone in place. We also think it will take a while to get settled, build the cabin and feel normal and we want to do that before the winter."

Jess moved over to put an arm around Harry – "It'll be a big adventure. We'll have loads of fun together exploring while Dad's working and then we can show him what we find at the weekends."

Harry smiled – it did sound exciting but then he thought about his friends at school, how he was going to leave them in 2 weeks time and not see them for ages. "Mum, what will happen about my friends? I won't see Karl and Bethany any more…" With that, a big tear rolled down Harry's cheek, followed by another one. He snuggled into Jess, who put her arm round him even tighter.

"Don't worry Harry, I know it doesn't feel easy right now and you're worried about your friends and your life here", she said, giving him a kiss on the head. "We're all going to miss people and it will be difficult to stay in touch to begin with. The phone signal isn't very strong and we won't have access to the Internet."

"WHAT?!", wailed Harry, pulling away from Jess and turning to look at her. "No Internet?" "How will we do anything?! I won't be able to chat with my friends or watch videos online. This is going to be awful!"

"It's alright Harry", Mark stepped in now. "I'll be getting a satellite phone which will let us make calls and send emails. It won't be the same but we can teach you how to email Karl and Bethany so you can stay in touch. Once the cabin is built and we've got solar panels working, we can get a proper Internet connection and that will make things feel more normal."

"Come on now, say good night to Dad, it's probably time for bed", Jess took Harry's hand and led him upstairs to clean his teeth. As Harry put on his pyjamas and got into bed, his mind was still whirling – 2 weeks until we leave to go to Canada and there won't be any Internet…

Chapter 2

Harry walked into the playground and immediately looked over to the corner of the field for his friend Karl. It was a new school term and the week after Mum and Dad had told him that they were moving to Canada. He hadn't seen Karl for what felt like ages and he was keen to talk to him about it.

"Bye, Mum", Harry said over his shoulder, turning at the last minute to give Jess a kiss and a hug.

"Bye, Harry, have a good day", replied Jess with a smile. She was walking with a group of mums and they headed towards the school gate, chatting together.

Harry ran across the field towards where he had spotted Karl playing football with a group of boys. "Hey Karl!", he shouted, "I've got something really cool to tell you!"

Karl passed the ball away and ran towards his excited friend. "Hi Harry, what's up?", he said with a grin. "Did you find the silver goalkeeper card?" The boys had been collecting football cards for a few months and everyone coveted the special silver ones.

"Oh no, it's way more exciting than that", replied Harry, slightly flushed with excitement and feeling a bit nervous too. "Mum and Dad told me in the holidays that we're moving to Canada. Dad's got a job looking after wildlife and we're going to live in a cabin in the woods!"

Karl stared at him in astonishment, his eyes widening and mouth slightly open. "What do you mean, Harry", he finally managed, "you're not going to be coming to school here any more?"

Harry suddenly felt sad – he hadn't thought of it like that before. It had seemed such an adventure – the idea of living in the woods and exploring everywhere but now he realised that all of the things he was used to would be changing too.

"It's ok, Karl", he said after a pause, "Dad says we can email each other and once we have the Internet, we'll be able to chat too."

"You. Won't. Have. The. Internet?!", Karl said slowly, with a confused look on his face. "What kind of place are you going to? The moon?"

What Harry was about to say was suddenly drowned out by the school bell and the friends found themselves in the middle of a noisy line of children queuing up to get into the classroom.

"Psst, Bethany!" Karl was trying to attract the girl's attention whilst Mr Morrison, their maths teacher was setting up the whiteboard.

Bethany turned in her chair to look at Karl and Harry who, as usual, were sat together and directly behind her. As she turned, her brown plaits flicked across the shoulder of her school t-shirt and Harry noticed that she had unicorn hair elastics in.

"Guess what?", Karl continued in a low voice, trying not to attract the teacher's attention. "Harry is moving to Canada to live in a cabin in the woods with no Internet!"

"Wow!", said Bethany, with a surprised look on her face. "That's not what I expected you two jokers to come out with this morning. When do you go Harry?"

"Yeah Harry, when do you go?", asked Karl, surprised at himself for not having asked already. The excitement of being told that morning hadn't worn off yet.

"We go next week", said Harry, "Mum and Dad told me in the holidays."

"So what's this about no Internet then?", Bethany asked. "How are we going to talk to each other?"

"Dad says where we will be living has a really poor phone signal", Harry explained, "but once we've got the cabin built they'll get the Internet put in. Dad says I can email to start with though but I don't know how to do that."

"Oh, that's no problem", Bethany smiled, "we can get Rob to help us." Rob was her older brother and in the top year at their school. "We'll find him at break and get him to explain it all."

"Rob!", Bethany shouted as the class piled out into the playground later and she spotted her brother. "Rob, come over here!"

"What's up Beth?", said Rob as he jogged over to the group, who by now were standing under a large tree in the corner of the playground.

"Harry's moving to Canada and we want you to tell us how to set up an email address so we can write to each other", explained Bethany. "He's going next week so we have to hurry!"

"Slow down", laughed Rob, "it's easy really – you just need to go onto the Webmail website and sign up for a free account. I'll write you some instructions and give them to Beth."

Harry smiled – maybe things weren't going to be so different after all. "Thanks Rob", he said as they turned to walk to the playing field together. Just then, Karl spotted a stray football on the edge of the playground and, with a shout, charged after it – the others trailing in his wake.

Later that week, Harry was walking home from school with Karl. It was a warm, sunny afternoon and the pair had taken their jumpers off and tied them around the straps of their rucksacks whilst they walked and talked. Harry had mixed feelings – excitement that he was about to go on a great adventure and sadness that he would be saying goodbye to his friends to do so. He put his hand in his pocket and felt the instructions on setting up an email address that Bethany had given him as she hugged him goodbye earlier. She had written her own email address in pink writing at the bottom and drawn a heart around it. Harry could feel tears pricking at his eyes but he didn't want Karl to see.

"Race you to the corner!", shouted Harry, taking off like he had been stung. Karl was close behind as they approached the row of trees at the corner of Harry's road. They both leaned over, panting at the effort and laughing. As Harry stood back up and looked in the direction of his house, he could see a large metal trailer parked on the drive with a big coloured sticker on the side.

"What's that?", asked Karl, following his line of vision. "Looks like some sort of container."

Harry felt a sinking feeling — the trailer was what they would be packing their things into to take to Canada. It all felt very real now.

"Come on mate, let's take a look", called Karl, setting off towards Harry's house.

As they got closer, the boys could both see the sticker on the side read 'D&D Transport'. "It's the removal van", said Harry quietly, "I guess this is it then."

"Hi Karl, hi love", Jess was waving to them from the drive as they approached. "How was your day at school?"

"It was fine mum, thanks", mumbled Harry.

Jess could see that Harry was upset at the sight of the removal trailer and came over to put her arm around his shoulders. "Did you get the instructions on setting up your email address?", she asked. "Emailing Karl and Bethany will help you feel like you're still here."

"Yeah, I've got them", said Harry, pulling the sheet of paper out of his pocket.

"Well let's sit down tonight and get that sorted for you", smiled Jess. "Karl – do you want to write your email address down on the sheet for Harry?"

Karl took the paper and pen which Jess had found in her pocket and scribbled a note at the bottom of the sheet. "Read it later", he said, trying to avoid eye contact. "I guess I'll be seeing you… or maybe not."

"Bye Karl, I'll email as soon as we get there", Harry was trying really hard not to cry now and waved as his friend walked back down the road, turning only once to wave back.

Jess put her arm around Harry and they walked into the house together.

"Mum…?", Harry began, "how are we going to fit all of our things into that trailer…?"

Chapter 3

The next day started with Harry waking early and running into his parents room.

"Mum, Dad, is it time to pack the trailer?", he asked excitedly.

Jess sat up, rubbing the sleep from her eyes and nudged Mark, who was doing his best to pretend to still be asleep.

"Yes it is, Harry", she replied with a smile, ruffling his hair as he slipped into bed between them.

Harry gave both his parents a big hug before sliding back out of the bed and disappearing as quickly as he'd arrived.

A little while later, when they'd showered and had breakfast, Harry started thinking about what he wanted to take to Canada with him. Mark had explained over breakfast that, as they were going to be living in a tent until their cabin was built, they'd have to take only essential items with them and the rest would go into storage.

"Dad", Harry called, "how much space will I have in the trailer?" He was suddenly worried about how many of his toys he'd be able to fit in.

Mark appeared with two large sports bags, one red and the other black. "Here you go Harry", he said, "one for your clothes and one for toys. Mum and I are doing the same."

"You're taking toys?", Harry asked in surprise. That didn't sound like his parents.

"No, no", laughed Mark, "we've got two bags too – one for clothes and the other for things to entertain us – books and stuff like that."

Harry took the two bags and set them down on his bed. Clothes seemed like less fun to sort out so he'd leave the black bag for them and think about his toys instead. He opened his toy cupboard and ran his eyes over the shelves inside. Books – he'd definitely need a few of them, toy cars – probably a couple; the yellow one and the blue sports car were his favourites, the dinosaur figures were probably too big and what about his castle and toy soldiers?

Footsteps sounded on the stairs and Jess walked in with some juice and a biscuit. "Here you go Harry", she said, handing them to him, "have you worked out which toys you're going to take yet?"

"I'm not sure Mum", Harry replied, "I want to take those books and the two cars but I can't decide between the other things in the cupboard – it's too hard."

"It's ok, Harry, I can't decide what to take either!", said Jess, sitting down on the floor beside him and looking over the toys on the shelves. She started to take items out one by one, with Harry nodding or shaking his head to signal which he'd prefer to take. Soon there was a pile of toys, books, board games and a football next to the red bag and Harry was feeling much happier. "Tell you what, you put them into the red bag and I'll help with your clothes", offered Jess.

"Thanks Mum", smiled Harry, picking up his things and carefully slotting them into the bag. When he had finished, he pulled the big silver zip all the way around the top of the bag and picked it up. "Ready to go!", he announced.

After lunch, Mark took Harry into the garden to practice putting their tent up. It was a new tent, made of bright orange fabric and had three big bedrooms plus a living area. The two of them had fun getting the poles in the right place and then Harry explored each of the bedrooms to see which one he wanted to have.

"Have you decided yet?", chuckled Mark. "You do know they're exactly the same?"

Harry wasn't bothered – he'd chosen the bedroom in the middle and that was where he was going to spend their first night under canvas in Canada.

"Harry! Mark! Granny and Grandad are here!", Jess was calling from the back door of the house. Harry's grandparents were coming over for tea to say goodbye and get some last minute lessons on sending email.

"Hi Harry, come for a hug!", Grandad appeared behind Jess at the door.

Harry ran over to hug both grandparents and then tugged them by the arm to look at the new tent. "Look, it has three bedrooms and loads of space inside. This one's my bedroom", he said, gesturing with his arm. "When we get to Canada, we're going to be sleeping in here until Dad has built the cabin."

"No pressure, Mark", smiled Granny as she looped her arm around her son. "We're going to miss you all. Once you've got the Internet it'll be easier and we can do that voice-calling thing."

"Yes, shouldn't be long", said Mark, "we reckon to be in the tent for a couple of months while we get enough of the cabin built to live in. Once we're at that stage, we can get power for the Internet."

The grown-ups sat down at the table for a chat before tea and Harry kicked a ball around the garden.

It seemed strange to think that tomorrow he'd be on an aeroplane, heading for a big adventure on the other side of the world and that new people would start living in his house.

Later that night, after a tea of sausage and mash, Granny and Grandad had gone home. There had been a few tears from them all at the thought of being apart for so long and Harry had hugged both grandparents extra hard before they got in the car. Mark had given his parents some print outs to remind them how to log onto their email account and what their new email address would be, along with some emergency contact details at the Canada Wildlife Trust who Mark would be working for.

Harry brushed his teeth, put his pyjamas on and got into bed for what would be the last time in this bedroom. Jess came in with a glass of water and to give him a goodnight cuddle.

"Well it's really here now Harry", she smiled as she handed the glass to him. "A man is coming to collect the trailer first thing tomorrow and then the taxi is coming, so you need to have a good long sleep."

"Mum", said Harry in a quiet voice, "I'm really going to miss everything – my room, all my things, Karl and Bethany…"

19

"I know", Jess put her arm around him and pulled him closer. "It's going to feel strange to begin with but you've got your favourite toys and you can email Karl and Bethany. We're going to have the best adventure ever – not something any of us had ever dreamed of a few months ago. Once we've been there a few days and started to settle in it will feel much more normal."

Harry snuggled into his mum's arm and wiggled his legs further under the covers. "Mm-hmm", he murmured sleepily, "love you Mum."

"I love you too, Harry", Jess said as she slowly got up from his bed, turned off the lamp and left the room, leaving Harry to dream of flying on a big shiny aeroplane high above the fluffy clouds.

Chapter 4

The next morning, after a breakfast of blueberry pancakes and yoghurt, Harry was watching the street out of the living room window. Jess had told him that a van was coming to collect the shiny silver trailer which had all of their things in and he didn't want to miss it. He had his blue sports car in one hand and was making it zoom over the carpet in front of the window. A few cars went by but it was mostly quiet outside.

"Mum", called Harry, "when's the van coming? I can't see it yet."

Jess walked into the room, carrying a tea towel and the bowl she was drying. "Soon, Harry", she said with a smile, "don't worry, you won't miss it."

Just then, there was a low growl from outside and the largest truck Harry had ever seen came down their road and pulled up outside the house. "Wow Mum, is that it? It's enormous", Harry exclaimed as he scrambled to his feet, his nose pressed against the window. He watched as the truck backed up to the trailer on the drive and then two hydraulic arms emerged and picked the trailer up into the air. Harry stared, his eyes wide, taking in the scene outside. "That's so cool Mum", was all he could say as the truck

21

driver carefully lowered the trailer onto the flatbed of the truck and strapped it down.

A few minutes later, after the truck had driven slowly away with Harry waving excitedly from the window, Mark came downstairs and into the room.

"Right, everything's off upstairs", he said, aiming a smile in Harry's direction. "The minibus will be here to take us to the airport soon, so let's get our bags put by the door."

Harry ran off to his room to pick up his red bag of toys which was sitting in the middle of his bed. He tried to lift the bag of clothes too, but decided it was too heavy. "Dad, can you help me with my clothes bag please?", he yelled as he walked down the stairs to put his bag by the front door with the others.

Before long, there was a ring at the door and the driver was helping to load their bags into the back of the minibus. Harry and Jess climbed through the sliding door to sit down whilst Mark locked the house and put the key in the key safe, ready for the people who were going to rent it to find later. Harry put his seatbelt on and then turned in his seat to wave goodbye to the house as they drove off down the road.

Once they arrived at the airport and Mark had found a big trolley to push their bags on, Harry was eager to explore. The airport had a big glass walled front and looked like something out of one of his superhero comics. Inside, there was a long row of check-in desks as far as he could see, all with different coloured signs above them.

"Let's get our bags checked in and then we can have a look around", suggested Mark. He looked at their tickets and pointed to a check-in desk half-way along on the left-hand side. He started to push the trolley and Harry wiggled under his arms to stand in front of his dad and help.

Once the bags had been checked in and Harry had asked where they went when they disappeared down a chute, Mark led the way to the security area. There was a slow-moving queue of people, taking turns to walk through a big metal arch which beeped occasionally. "That's an X-ray machine", Jess told Harry, "it checks to see if you have anything you're not allowed to take on the plane." As they approached the metal arch, Mark and Jess both put their carry bags into plastic trays and put them into a machine next to the arch. "It's another X-ray machine", explained Jess.

Mark went through the metal arch and then turned to wave Harry to come through. As he passed under it, there was a loud beep and Harry jumped. "Can you come over here please?", said a man in uniform next to the arch.

"It's ok", said Mark, moving closer to Harry as Jess took her turn to come through the arch. Harry was a bit scared but bravely stepped towards the man who waved what looked like a switched off torch across his front. 'Beep' went the torch, as it passed over Harry's waist.

"Are you wearing a belt?", asked the man. "Would you mind showing me?" As Harry lifted his top to reveal a belt with a metal buckle, the man smiled. "That's ok, thank you. It's important for us to check", he said as he waved Harry back over to his parents.

After stopping for some sandwiches for lunch, it was time to head to the boarding gate to find their plane. Harry was amazed to see a corridor of people moving along but standing still! "It's a travelator", said Mark with a smile, "like an escalator but flat. It saves having to walk." Well, this was great from Harry's point of view – he ran over to it and stood holding the side rail as the moving floor carried him along the corridor. Jess and Mark followed, chuckling at Harry's excitement, until they reached the end of the travelator and a large section of purple seats.

"It's a plane!", shouted Harry in excitement, rushing over and pressing his nose against the window for the second time that day.

"It's our plane", laughed Mark as he joined Harry at the window. "Look, there are 4 big engines and two rows of windows – that's because there are two floors of seats, just like a double decker bus."

"Which ones are we sitting on?", asked Harry. "I hope it's at the front."

"Oh Harry!", laughed Jess, "you can't see out of the windows at the front – they're for the pilots. You get to look out of the side windows."

They joined the growing queue of people waiting to get on the plane and, after showing their tickets and walking down a long tunnel, found themselves at the plane door.

"Welcome to Air Canada", said a smiling stewardess as she checked their tickets again. "Your seats are half-way along on the right."

Harry had memorised the seat numbers on the tickets his dad was holding – 43 A, B and C. He found them and sat down excitedly in the window seat.

Before long, the pilot had asked everyone to put their seat belts on and started to slowly taxi the plane towards the runway. Jess gave Harry a sweet to suck for take-off and offered her hand for him to hold. "It can be a bit noisy when you first take off", she said, as he put his hand in hers. There was a sudden roar from the engines and Harry felt a big shove backwards in his seat as the plane sped down the runway. It was suddenly quiet and the front of the plane tipped upwards. "We're in the air now", smiled Jess, "the adventure has begun."

Harry was amazed at the choice of TV channels on the plane and spent several happy hours before and after dinner was served watching cartoons and a funny film with a clown in. As it got dark outside, the stewardesses brought blankets round and Harry snuggled into his seat for a sleep.

"This is your captain speaking..." Harry awoke with a start and rubbed his eyes. "We will shortly be descending into Toronto International Airport." As the announcement finished, Harry looked out of the window. It was getting light and there was a vast area of forest beneath them, slowly giving way to houses and roads. Harry could start to see cars moving far below them, looking like ants running about in long lines.

"Well Harry, we're here", smiled Mark, "it's going to be amazing."

Chapter 5

As they filed through the plane towards the door, Harry peered out of the window. It was grey – the concrete beneath the plane, the sky and the tunnel snaking out from the airport building to join up with the plane door. Harry wondered to himself what kind of place this would turn out to be – more interesting than just grey he hoped.

"Thank you for flying Air Canada", the steward at the door said to Mark and Jess as they passed. As Harry walked up to him, he bent down slightly. "Give me 5!", he said to Harry, smiling as he held his hand up. Harry slapped his palm, grinned and walked through the doorway into Canada.

After what seemed like an endless walk through the airport – there were no travelators, which was a bad thing in Harry's mind already – they got to the baggage reclaim area. Mark went over to a large TV screen and came back moments later pointing to a carousel in the middle of the room.

"It's over here guys, screen says it'll be 5 minutes until the bags start to come off", he explained. "Why is it called a carousel?", Harry asked, "it doesn't look much like the ones at the fair."

Jess chuckled to herself as she replied – "Wait until it starts up Harry, then you'll see! Just don't ride on it", she added, after a moment's hesitation. "That man over there won't like it."

Harry turned and saw a large man in police uniform walking through the airport. The policeman saw Harry staring and gave a smile before saying something into his radio and heading off towards the exit.

"Here we go!", exclaimed Mark excitedly. "The bags are coming." First to come out was a large red suitcase, seemingly only held together with bright yellow tape. It toppled onto its side and started to move along the carousel. A small boy rushed towards it excitedly but then stopped as he realised it wasn't his case.

A long stream of cases, bags and pushchairs passed in front of them, before Mark quickly stepped forward and picked up a holdall, soon followed by Harry's red bag. It wasn't long until all of their bags were in a pile at their feet and Jess was loading them onto a trolley, ready to push them out of the airport. They walked towards the exit together and Harry saw a long line of people, some holding signs, and others looking excitedly into the slow stream of people emerging with their trolleys of luggage.

"Look Dad, that sign has our name on it!", Harry turned excitedly to Mark. "How strange is that?" Mark pointed the trolley towards the man with the sign; Harry and Jess following.

"Hi, I'm Mark Jones", said Mark to the man.

"Nice to meet you, I'm Tim", came the response. "I'm with the Canada Wildlife Trust. The truck's outside, all ready to go."

When they got outside, Harry was amazed to see a shiny red pickup truck with the trailer he had last seen outside their house hitched up to the back. Seeing his surprise, Tim explained – "The trailer was on an earlier flight – I picked it up right before I came to meet you."

Harry and Jess climbed into the back seat of the pickup and Mark got into the front alongside Tim. Harry was feeling tired and excited at the same time. "How long will it take us to get there?", he asked Tim.

"Probably six hours or so", came the reply. "About as long as you were on the plane for and I'm afraid I don't have any movies."

Harry settled into the corner of his seat as they pulled away from the airport. He still had his blue sports car and started driving it over the seat, across the door and up the window. At first, it was exciting looking out of the window – everything looked the same as at home, yet different. All the cars were slightly different shapes and the shop signs were different colours but it still felt a bit familiar.

After half an hour of staring at the world passing by outside, Harry yawned and felt his eyes start to shut. "That's it Harry, have a nap", said Jess. "It's a long way and you'll be bored otherwise." Harry drifted off to the sound of his dad talking to Tim about the Wildlife Trust and the work that they were doing.

Harry woke to the crunch of tyres on gravel. He opened his eyes and could see that the houses had been replaced by trees – lots of trees. Everywhere he looked there were tall pine trees and green bushes nearer ground level. The truck slowed down as it entered a clearing in the trees and then pulled to a halt. Suddenly everything was quiet as Tim turned the engine off and they opened the doors.

Harry clambered out excitedly. The first thing he noticed was the air – there was a sweet smell being borne along by the gentle breeze. The second thing he noticed was that there nothing in the clearing apart from the truck and its trailer. "Dad...", Harry started, "where's the cabin?"

"We have to build it", smiled Mark. "Don't worry, we brought the tent to start with, don't you

31

remember?"

"Build it from what?", asked Harry. There was nothing except trees as far as he could see.

"Here you go", said Tim, walking round and opening the load bay of the pickup. "There's all the tools you need here and more." He lifted out a chainsaw and large workbench and then he and Mark dragged a wooden crate out and set it on the ground. "That's everything you'll need for the first couple of nights", he said, "we'll arrange another drop in a day or two and set you up a storage shed for your tools."

"We can use the trailer to start with, once we've unloaded it", Mark explained, unhitching it and setting the tow bar down on the stand. He opened the door at the back of the trailer and pulled out their tent and a small camping stove. "It was a good idea to put these in last, wasn't it?", he smiled.

After Tim had gone, Mark, Jess and Harry started to put the tent up. It was more Mark and Jess but Harry enjoyed getting the poles out and pinging them together on their elastic rope. Once the tent was up, Jess opened the camping stove and then produced a packet of sausages from inside the crate.

"Yay, sausages!", shouted Harry excitedly, then ran in circles around the clearing whilst the sizzling on the stove gave way to a delicious smell of tea. They sat on the top of the crate to eat, looking at their surroundings and trying to take it all in.

"Mum, I need the loo", said Harry suddenly. "Where is it?" He looked around nervously – "There is a loo, isn't there?"

"Yes, and it's a very clever loo too", Mark explained as he went to the back of the trailer and produced a large blue cardboard box. "It's a compost toilet. It turns all the yucky stuff we put into it back into good soil which plants love."

"Wow", said Harry, "can I use it now please? I'm desperate!"

Mark got the compost toilet out of the box and sprinkled a little moss from underneath the nearest tree into it. "There you go, Harry", he said. "We'll put a little tent around it tomorrow."

After he had used the toilet and brushed his teeth with some bottled water from the crate, Harry put on his pyjamas and unrolled his sleeping bag. He put it into the middle bedroom of the tent and wriggled in. "Night Mum, night Dad", he called and then put his head on his pillow and settled down for his first night's sleep in the wilderness.

Chapter 6

'SCRAPE..... SCRAPE.....'

Harry sat up with a start – what was that funny noise?

There it was again – 'scrape.... scraaaaaaaaaaaaaaape' – quieter this time but it still sounded like it was right next to his head.

Harry unzipped his sleeping bag and peered around the bedroom pod. It was almost dark but with a faint yellow edge to the light. He fumbled for the zip and slowly undid it – 'zzzzzzzzzzzzzzzz'.

"Harry, is that you?", Mark called softly from the pod next door.

"Mm hmm", answered Harry. "There's a strange noise outside."

Mark unzipped the door of his bedroom pod and knelt to get out. "Keep it quiet and we'll try not to wake Mum." He moved to the front zip of the tent and listened. "I can't hear anything but let's check it out anyway."

As he slipped his feet into the shoes Mark had gently thrown over to him, Harry wondered what the creature or person outside was and what they had been doing. "I'm a bit scared Dad", he whispered.

Mark slid the front zip open, ducked out of the tent and then put a hand back in for Harry to take. They stood up, getting used to the half light, then Mark led the way slowly around the tent. Suddenly, there was a loud scrabbling noise and the crashing of twigs as something ran away from the tent. Harry jumped, tugging on Mark's hand, who in turn quickly switched on the torch that he was carrying in his other hand, just in time to spot an animal about the size of a small pony but with horns running away.

"Was that a deer?", asked Harry, his voice slightly high with excitement. "It looked like one with those horns."

"No, I think that was a moose, Harry", replied Mark. "They're a bit like a deer but they live in Canada and a few other places. That was probably a young one looking for food."

"Cool", said Harry, "do you think we'll see any more?"

Mark chuckled quietly, "I'm sure we will Harry. That's what living out in the wilderness is like – plenty of wildlife on your doorstep all the time." He walked over to the spot where the moose had been standing and looked at the ground. "Cheeky thing", he said, "it looks like it was trying to paw it's way into the tent."

"Would it have got in?", Harry asked, a little scared again.

"No, the tent material is very tough although it feels thin." Mark was running his hand over the side of the tent, feeling for any damage. "I think it could probably smell the leftover sausages that we wrapped up from tea and put in the spare bedroom pod. We won't make that mistake again!"

"Mmm, sausages", said Harry, "how soon until breakfast?"

Mark looked at his watch – "It's half past four, Harry – you've got a little while yet!" He looked at the tent some more and then the ground in front of it where there was the beginning of a small hole. "I think we ought to put up some moose barriers before we go back to bed – are you up for it?"

"Sure", came the reply, "but can I have a torch too?" As Mark went to retrieve a spare torch from the tent, Harry gazed around him. It was so quiet out here and in the dim light he could make out the shapes of some of the trees, silhouetted against the dark sky. It felt a bit creepy but so exciting too.

Mark came back and passed Harry a torch – "Try not to shine it on the tent", he advised, "let's try and avoid disturbing Mum." He walked over to the tree line with

Harry – "Look for some big sticks, the straighter the better", he said, pointing out something suitable with his torch beam.

"Here's one!", Harry exclaimed, "is this ok?" He was brandishing a long stick with a sharp looking pointy end.

"That's great", said Mark quietly, "just remember that we're trying not to wake Mum!"

After 10 minutes of hunting, they had a big pile of sticks lying beside the tent and Harry wondered what was coming next. "What do we do with them now Dad", he asked, "are we going to make a moose trap?"

"Ha ha! No Harry, we're going to make a moose fence", laughed Mark. "You take the sticks like this and push them into the ground close together." He demonstrated with a few sticks and then let Harry join in until they had a ring around the back half of the tent. "Now we're going to pull some of the smaller leaves from that tree over there and spread them around in front of the fence. Moose like to eat them and they'll soon forget that we're here if we leave a tasty treat for them."

Harry joined in pulling small bunches of leaves from the lower branches of the tree and sprinkling them in

37

front of the new fence. "What are these leaves called, Dad?", he asked.

"They're birch leaves", replied Mark. "Moose really like them as they're low in fibre and they can digest them easily." Sometimes it can be handy having a wildlife ranger for a Dad!

Once the leaves had been sprinkled, Harry began to yawn. "I think I'm ready for bed again", he said, sleepily. "Will we have to do this every night?"

"No", laughed Mark, "we'll make a proper barrier over the next few days and once the cabin's built they won't bother us. He just smelled something different and came to investigate."

"Maybe move the sausages too?", suggested Harry. "I could eat them for you if you haven't got anywhere to put them?"

"Thanks, but no thanks", came the reply. "I think we can find space for them in the trailer where they'll be nice and safe and the moose may not be able to smell them either." Mark ducked inside the tent and came back with a foil parcel in his hand.

"Crikey Dad, no wonder the moose came to investigate, I can smell them from here", Harry said with a grin. "Are you sure I can't have one?"

"Not if you want any left for breakfast", Mark said, walking over to the trailer. He patted his pocket — "Oh no, I've left the key in the tent."

"I'll get it", said Harry, lifting the flap and disappearing inside. There was a bit of shuffling and then he reappeared with the key swinging from its yellow fob. He passed it to Mark, who unlocked the trailer door and slid the foil parcel inside, before locking it again.

"There you go, all safe for breakfast", he said. "Come on, let's get you back to bed now before it's too light."

They stepped back inside the tent together and sat side by side on the floor taking their shoes off. "This is really exciting Dad", Harry whispered. "Much more fun than being at home."

Mark smiled — "I'm so pleased you think so Harry. Mum and I weren't sure if you'd like it — being away from all your friends and everything."

"I can email them and once we've got the Internet I can talk to them on that", Harry replied. "It's no big deal." He stood up — "Can I have a drink though before I go back to bed please?"

"There's water in the big bottle on the table", suggested Mark, "or a bit of milk in the cold box."

"Water's fine", Harry replied as he walked over and poured himself a small glass.

"Definitely time for bed now", smiled Mark as he opened up Harry's bedroom pod door and held it up so Harry could get in. "Night, Harry!", he said as he quietly pulled the zip up.

"Night Dad... again!", came the reply.

Chapter 7

Harry woke up later that morning to the smell of sausages. Briefly, he wondered if the moose was back but then he realised it was light and he could hear his parents talking outside the tent. He clambered out of his pod and through the open front flap of the tent.

"Hi Mum, hi Dad", he called.

"Hi love", Jess replied, looking up from the camping stove. "Dad tells me you had quite an adventure last night whilst I was asleep?"

"It was fun, wasn't it, Harry?", Mark chipped in. He was sitting across from Jess, stirring a cup of coffee.

"We saw a moose and it was trying to get into the tent to eat our sausages", Harry chattered excitedly. "We had to make a fence to stop it coming back."

"I saw it", said Jess, smiling. "It looks very good."

Harry sat down next to his dad — "What's for breakfast?", he asked.

"Sausages — what else?", replied Mark, laughing and giving Harry a hug.

As Harry tucked into his breakfast, he looked around the clearing again — there were a lot of very tall trees and most of them seemed to have birds perched in them. "It's nice here", he remarked between mouthfuls.

"We really wanted to spend some time somewhere peaceful", Jess explained. "This was too good a chance for us to turn down – being away from noise and cars and spending time in the lovely clean air."

Harry cleared his plate and held it out for a second helping, his thoughts turning to the day ahead. "What are we doing today?", he asked. "Are we going to be exploring the woods?"

"Well", Mark answered him, "there's a river about half a mile away, through the trees. I thought we could have a look over there and see if we can see any more animals."

"That sounds great", Harry said excitedly. "What kind of animals do they have in Canada?"

"All the regular ones you're used to", replied Mark, "plus moose of course, bears in some areas and beavers."

"I really want to see a bear", Harry exclaimed, "a really big one!"

Mark chuckled – "Bears can be very dangerous", he explained, "they're not like teddies at all – if we see one, we'll need to keep well away from it."

After breakfast, Harry asked about having a shower. "We've not set the portable shower up yet", Mark said. "It's solar powered, so we need the sun to warm the water during the day before we can really use it." He then opened the trailer and took out a large black box – "Here it is", he said, "we just need to hang it up on the side of the trailer and let the sun do its thing."

"Ok", said Harry, "what should I do about washing?"

"Just use some water from the bottle on your flannel for now and wash your hands and face", suggested Jess. "You can have a shower this evening."

Harry went to get his flannel and tipped some water onto it. He screwed it into a ball and wiped his face. "Brrr!", he said, "it's really cold." He then washed his hands with soap and some more water from the bottle before drying himself on a towel that Jess had given him. "Just going to get dressed", he announced, then went back into the tent to choose some clothes for the day.

When Harry poked his head out of the tent again, he saw that Mark had taken a big rucksack out of the trailer and was packing it with things. "What are you doing?", he asked.

"I'm just getting a few things ready for our mini adventure", Mark replied. "You never know what you might find out here so we need some essentials. I've got a radio in case of emergencies, a first aid kit and a bear alarm."

"What's a bear alarm?", asked Harry.

"Well it basically makes a very loud noise if you press it", Mark explained. "The idea is that if you meet a bear then you can frighten it away so that it doesn't hurt you." He explained to Harry that some people carry a gun to either frighten off or shoot the bear in an emergency but that, as a conservationist, he didn't think it was a good idea.

"Can I have a go?", Harry said, eyeing up the bear alarm.

"No", Mark said firmly – "we don't want to scare any wildlife unless we think we're in danger. We're here to observe them and look after them, not to upset them."

"Are we ready then?", asked Jess. She had disappeared inside the tent whilst Mark and Harry were talking and now had a bag of her own and was wearing a waterproof jacket. She held one out to Harry to put on.

"Is it going to rain?", asked Harry, "it looks sunny to me."

"You never know out here", replied Jess, "the weather can change a lot when you're in the forest so let's be prepared."

They walked towards the edge of the clearing, roughly in the direction the moose had disappeared in last night, with Mark leading the way and Harry walking alongside Jess, talking excitedly.

After about 5 minutes, they came to another clearing – this one smaller than the one which their tent was pitched in. Mark stopped – "Let's check for animal markings", he said.

"What do you mean?", asked Harry.

Mark produced a small book from his pocket and passed it to Harry. It had page after page of animal footprints in. "If we can spot some footprints and identify them", he said, "that will let us know what kind of animals are living round here."

Harry pointed to a footprint which looked a lot like a human foot but with claw marks at the end. "What's that one, Dad?", he asked.

"I'm pretty sure that's a badger", Mark answered, showing Harry the right page in the book. "They live in tunnels underground called setts."

After looking around for a few moments more, they continued in the same direction. Harry started to play 'I-Spy', choosing different coloured leaves on the various trees for his guesses.

Suddenly, the sound of water could be heard. "I think we're almost at the river now", Mark announced. "We just need to be careful as it sounds like its flowing quite fast." They walked a few metres further and Harry glimpsed blue through the trees.

"It's the river!", he shouted in excitement and tugged Jess by the hand. The river was a gorgeous blue colour and, set against the trees on the far bank, it looked magical.

"Let's see what we can spot", suggested Jess, as Mark got out a notepad and started jotting things down. She walked a bit closer to the river with Harry and they both stared into the water.

"Do you think we'll see some big fish?", asked Harry. "I'd like fish for my tea!"

"I'm not sure about that", chuckled Jess, "but look over there." She crouched down and pointed along the riverbank. Harry followed the direction of her finger with his eye but couldn't see what she was pointing at.

"What is it, Mum?", he asked.

"Look down by the side of the river — small and brown", replied Jess. Harry looked and then he saw it — a brown beaver swimming along by an old log. He knew it was a beaver because he could see its flat tail when it flicked into a dive and disappeared briefly under the water.

"Wow", said Harry, "what is it doing?"

"See that log?", Jess asked, "it's called a lodge. That's basically where the beaver lives — most of it is behind the log in the pile of sticks but the entrance is underwater which is why he keeps diving." The beaver appeared again, swimming up the river and returning with a small branch in its mouth. "He's gone out to get food for some babies", explained Jess. "They just have milk when they're first born but they move on to branches and leaves pretty quickly."

Mark appeared next to them — "Sorry to disturb the nature lesson", he said, "but there's a quad bike being delivered in a bit and we should be back when they get there."

"That's so cool!", said Harry, "our own quad bike. Will I get to have a go?"

"Maybe on the back sometimes", said Mark with a smile. "Let's get going."

The walk back to the tent was uneventful – they saw several woodpeckers high up in trees and making their distinctive 'tap-tapping' sound but no animals at ground level. When they arrived in the clearing, they saw a familiar face standing outside his pickup truck.

"Tim!", said Harry excitedly, "and you've brought our quad bike." He raced over to the pickup and stared at the bright blue machine. It had a long dark blue seat and lighter blue bodywork. On the front was a luggage rack and it looked like a lot of fun.

"Hi Tim", Mark greeted the man warmly, "thanks for dropping this off – it'll make getting about a lot easier."

"No problem", said Tim, "there's a few big cans of gas in the back too and if you head 10 miles or so back down the track there's a gas station in the first village." He paused and noticed Harry looking quizzically at him – "I think you call it petrol", he explained, "we call it gas – same thing though."

Mark helped Tim to roll the quad bike down a ramp off the pickup and pushed it over next to the trailer. "Would you like to stay for a drink, Tim?", he offered.

"Thanks, I'll do that", replied Tim.

As the grown-ups sat and drank coffee outside the tent, Harry clambered onto the seat of the quad bike and pretended he was driving it fast through the forest.

He made all the noises and leaned into pretend corners on his imaginary ride. He was sure this was going to be so much fun to go on for real.

Chapter 8

"Mum, where's my helmet?", Harry called as he rummaged through the open trailer door. He'd seen his dad put a box with three new helmets inside into the trailer last night but now he couldn't see them.

"Just inside the tent door, Harry", Jess called. She was finishing off a picnic lunch for them – putting sandwiches and crisps into a small cold bag zipped onto the top of one of their rucksacks.

"Found it", Harry emerged with a shiny blue helmet on his head, his fingers fumbling with the chin strap. "How do I do this up Mum?", he asked.

Jess put the last few things into the cold bag and walked over to Harry. She knelt down and adjusted the strap, holding Harry's fingers to show him by touch how to fasten it. "There you go, you look ready to roll", she announced. "Just a few more things to pack and we'll be ready to go." Mark had gone out earlier to set some hidden wildlife cameras up near the riverbank they had walked to yesterday and Jess was going to take Harry out exploring on the quad bike.

"Why did Dad have to go and do work things?", asked Harry.

"Well, that's kind of why we're here", laughed Jess. "His job is to look after and study the wildlife and, nice as it is to go off and explore, he really needs to start helping the other conservation rangers." She zipped up the tent door and swung the rucksack over her shoulder – "Right, are you ready to go?"

Harry climbed onto the back of the quad bike seat behind his mum and put his arms around her waist. The rucksack was strapped to the luggage rack on the front and Harry was super excited. 'Whir, whir, grrrrr' – the quad bike's engine started up and Harry squeezed Jess tighter.

"Ok Harry?", Jess shouted over her shoulder.

"Yes!", Harry shouted back, and the quad bike slowly pulled out of the clearing with Jess heading further up the dirt track.

It was really bouncy on the back of the quad bike and Harry could feel every bump – not in a painful way but more like being on a trampoline with other people bouncing you about. Harry looked to his side and saw bushes whizzing past as they wound their way up the hill, turning this way and that as the track got steeper.

After about 20 minutes, Jess pulled into the side of the track and turned off the engine. She pulled off her helmet and turned to Harry – "If I read the map right this morning then there's something very exciting to show you just through here."

Harry jumped off the seat and pulled his own helmet off – "What is it, Mum?"

"Well, I'll give you a clue", Jess smiled. She opened the rucksack and took out a pair of binoculars. "I think you might be needing these", she said.

Harry took the binoculars excitedly and put the strap around his neck. Jess offered him her hand and they walked along a little path which Harry hadn't noticed before. It looked like it was used by small animals more than people as it was so narrow and only a thin strip of earth was worn away through the grass.

"How far is it?", Harry asked. "Will we have our lunch there?"

"Not far now", replied Jess, "a couple of minutes probably. We won't have lunch there as we don't want to scare any birds – I've got another idea for that."

They rounded a big tree and Harry saw their destination – a wooden bird hide, partly covered in camouflage netting. Quietly, they went inside the hide and Harry could see there were little windows with hatches over them that you could lower to watch the birds outside.

"Mum", he whispered, "do you have that bird book?"

Smiling, Jess handed it to him – "You don't think I'd forget that, do you Harry?"

Harry put the binoculars to his face and studied the sky. He couldn't see anything, so moved his gaze down to the trees and concentrated hard. Suddenly, he heard a 'bee-bee-be' song coming from the right of the hide and swung the binoculars around to look. There was a little sandy coloured bird with a black head singing in a tree close to the hide.

"Can you help me find out what it is please, Mum?", Harry asked quietly. He passed her the book without taking his eyes away from the tiny bird in the tree.

"I think with a song like that, it's probably a chickadee", said Jess. She thumbed through the book to check. "Is that what you can see?", she asked Harry, holding out a page to him.

Harry reluctantly lowered the binoculars for a second – "Yes, that looks like it", he confirmed. "How did you know, Mum?"

"I had a lot of time to read on the plane whilst you were asleep", Jess explained. "Besides, the song is very much like a blue tit, and we have loads of those back at home."

After another 15 minutes or so of scanning the sky and trees but failing to spot any more birds, Harry announced that he was getting hungry. "That's fine", agreed Jess, "so am I." She led them out of the hide and back along the path towards where they had parked the quad bike.

"Are we going back now?", asked Harry. "I thought we might have lunch somewhere fun."

"Don't you worry, Harry", Jess told him, "I've got just the place." They took a turning off to the left which wound its way around a huge boulder and then they emerged from the trees to a stunning view. They were facing the river which they had walked to the day before, only much higher up and they could see for miles. Harry traced the track part of the way down the hill with his finger, before giving up as it disappeared into the tree line.

"Is this ok for you?", Jess asked, putting a picnic blanket down on the ground and unzipping the cold bag. "There's cheese sandwiches, crisps, apples and some orange squash."

"Thanks Mum", Harry replied, as he picked up a sandwich and started munching.

"If you look down there, past that really tall tree by the rock", Jess pointed with her finger, "that's about where the tent is." Harry looked – it seemed a really long way down.

"I wonder if we'll see Dad from up here", Harry wondered aloud.

"I think he might be a bit too far away", Jess said, "maybe we'll ask him to wear something really bright next time we come up here to make it easier."

As they ate, they pointed out more things in the view to each other – the houses at the edge of the village far below, a rock that looked like a monster (that was Harry's one) and where the river seemed to flow into the sky, far away on the horizon.

"Shall we explore up here a bit more?", Jess asked when they had finished. "I think there's probably some caves in that big rock we passed." She led the way back along the path, having made sure all of their picnic was cleared away – "Can't leave litter out here, it would spoil the beauty."

"Look Mum, there is a cave!", Harry shouted excitedly. He tugged on Jess's arm and pulled her towards it.

"Just be careful, Harry", Jess warned. "We don't know what's inside and we might scare something living in there." She pulled two torches out of her rucksack and gave one to Harry. Slowly, they walked towards the cave and peered in, their torches making shadows dance on the walls. The cave was huge and the torchlight wasn't really bright enough to see much so, after going a few more paces inside, Jess stopped Harry. "I don't think we should go much further today, Harry. We can come back with Dad and a more powerful torch another day."

"Ok", said Harry. He was torn – he really wanted to explore further inside the cave but it was a bit dark and his mum was probably right. Plus, if Mark came with them then Harry would have two hands to hold if it got really scary! He shone his torch beam over the side wall of the cave as he turned to leave, then stopped. He was sure he had seen a pair of eyes looking back at him.

"Mum, look over here", Harry said softly, as he swung his torch back in the direction of the eyes. Nothing - just inky blackness staring back at him. He swung the torch in a few more arcs but still couldn't see the eyes he was sure were watching him.

"It could have been an owl, I suppose", suggested Jess. "They do nest in caves sometimes and are mostly nocturnal." She led Harry out of the cave and back into

the bright sunlight. Harry was sure that he'd seen an
owl but there was no way of knowing now. They'd just
have to come back again soon.

Chapter 9

The next morning, Harry was sitting outside the tent on one of the folding chairs, looking with some trepidation at a large brown envelope. Inside was the pack of schoolwork his teacher had given him on his last day. It was meant to keep him busy until they had access to the Internet and could sign up for some online lessons.

"Mum....", Harry began, "do I have to do this today?" He wasn't excited by the thought of school when there was so much to explore around them.

"Unfortunately, you do", came the reply. "It's really important to learn, Harry, and we can't teach you everything. Dad and I know quite a bit about wildlife but not anywhere near as much as you need to learn about other things."

Harry reluctantly opened the envelope and shook the contents out. He turned over the pack of paper that emerged and sighed – spellings... Not his favourite.

"Come on Harry", Jess said encouragingly, "do an hour's work and then we can do something else."

"Ok", muttered Harry and picked up the green pencil that his teacher had also thoughtfully put into the envelope. He worked through two pages of spellings – they were ones he'd learnt in his last weeks at school and he managed to do them quite easily. Next, he turned to the maths section and groaned – not fractions! He didn't think it could get any worse after spellings...

Jess noticed Harry's lack of enthusiasm and came over to see what was up. "I used to like fractions at school", she said, "it always made more sense when you multiplied them so that the numbers on the bottom were the same."

"Thanks Mum", replied Harry, "I'd forgotten that bit." He looked at the exercise again, wrote a few numbers on the sheet and sat back – "Are these right?", he asked.

Jess checked the answer page at the back – "Yep", she answered, "well done Harry – that wasn't so hard, was it?" She stood up and walked over to the tent door – "Tell you what, you do another page whilst I make lunch and then we'll leave it for today. Deal?"

"Deal", replied Harry as he picked up his pencil again.

Just as Jess returned with some sandwiches on a big plate, Harry heard the roar of a quad bike and jumped up as Mark rode into the clearing. "Dad!", he yelled, running over to him – "you're back!"

Mark turned the engine off and dismounted. As he pulled his helmet off, he smiled and ruffled Harry's hair. "How's the schoolwork going?", he asked.

"A bit boring, but I've done some spellings and some maths this morning", answered Harry. "Look, I can show you."

Mark took the pack and looked through the pages – "That's great, Harry, good work." He fished in his pocket and brought out a small envelope – "I've got a surprise for you", he said, as he handed it to Harry.

Harry took the envelope and looked at it. He didn't recognise the writing but the postmark said 'England' on it so it must be someone at home. Tearing open the top, he pulled out two sheets of paper. "It's Karl and Bethany!", he said excitedly – "they've written to me."

"That's lovely", Jess told him, "I wonder how they knew where to write to?"

"Ah", Mark said, tapping his nose. Smiling, he told them that he had given Karl and Bethany's parents the postal box address that he planned to use for work letters. "I thought it would be nice for Harry to get a surprise letter when we arrived", he explained.

"They're asking how the journey was and what the campsite is like", said Harry. "I don't think they realise how far out in the woods we're living."

"Well you can write back this afternoon if you like?", Mark offered, "I've got to go down into the village again later so we could go together and post it."

"Really?", asked Harry, a big grin on his face. "That would be ace!"

"And now it's time for lunch", laughed Jess. They all sat down and ate their sandwiches as Mark told them about his morning. He had been to check the post as he was expecting a satellite phone to be delivered but it hadn't arrived yet.

"Is there much in the village?", asked Jess. "We could do with a bit more food – some tins of things as they'll keep better."

"There's a petrol station, a post office and a small general store", Mark answered, "not much else apart from houses and not many of those to be honest. I'll pick some bits up later if you like?"

After lunch, Harry pulled out a sheet of paper and began to write. 'To Karl and Bethany', he wrote first – he was having to write one letter to them both as only Karl had included his address in the letters to Harry. Two pages and a lot of small handwriting later, Harry had explained just about everything he'd done since arriving.

61

"Have you written enough?", joked Jess, as she looked over at Harry's page. "You can write to them as often as you like. Dad will be going into the village several times a week so it won't be a problem getting to the post office."

Harry folded his letter in half and half again, before sliding it into the white envelope Jess put on the table in front of him. "I've written Karl's address on it for you", she explained. "You just need Dad to buy a stamp in the post office."

"When can we post it?", asked Harry.

"I'll be heading out in about an hour", replied Mark. "I just need to check on the hidden cameras that I put down near the river yesterday."

Almost exactly an hour later, Mark returned, whistling quietly to himself as he walked back into the clearing. "Come on then, Harry", he called, "let's pop down to the village whilst they're still likely to be open."

The ride on the quad bike wasn't quite as big an adventure as his first time yesterday but Harry still felt excited to be on the back, arms wrapped around his dad and with the wind tugging at him as they passed gaps in the trees. It was nearly half an hour's ride before they spotted the first houses in the village appearing through the trees. Mark turned right at the bottom of the track, where it met the road, and then drove on through the village until they came to the post office.

"Let's do your letter first", he suggested, "then we'll look for some food in the general store." As they entered the post office, past the blue and red sign, the first thing Harry noticed was how quiet it was.

"There aren't many people about, are there Dad?", he asked.

The lady behind the counter smiled at Harry – "We don't get many tourists here", she said. "Where are you two from?"

"We're from England", explained Mark. "I've got a job with the Wildlife Trust and we're building a cabin up in the woods."

"Oh, that sounds exciting", the lady replied, "it'll be a great adventure for you." She took the envelope that Harry placed on the counter and asked if he needed a stamp.

"Yes please, for England", Harry said. "It's for my friends from school – Karl and Bethany."

"Well I bet you've had loads to tell them", smiled the lady as she stuck the stamp on and put the envelope into a mailbag beside her. "That will be $2.50 please."

Mark handed her the money – "Thank you", he said, "I'm sure we'll be seeing you again."

Harry waved as they headed out of the post office and into the general store across the road. "What do you fancy for tea?", Mark asked as they gazed at rows of tinned food. Harry scanned the shelves and pulled out a tin. "You can't have sausages again!", laughed Mark, "we need to have a balanced diet." He got a basket and chose a selection of soups, stews and some tinned fruit.

"Can we get some more bread?", Harry suggested. "I think I saw it near the back of the shop." They walked around the shelves and found the bread – Harry choosing two seeded loaves and some small rolls.

At the checkout, Mark packed the food into his rucksack – "Better hope this lot fits on the luggage rack", he joked. "We don't want Mum to find it's all squashed when we get back!" Harry smiled at his dad as he helped pick up the last few bits – even going to the shops was fun on this exciting adventure!

As they rode back up the track, Harry thought he could feel all of the bumps in the ground underneath their wheels. Suddenly, there was a bigger lurch to the side and Mark braked sharply – the quad bike coming to rest, leaning at a crazy angle.

"What's happened?", exclaimed Harry, pushing the visor of his helmet up to make himself heard.

"We've got a puncture", Mark said slowly. "It looks like a nasty one too."

"What are we going to do?", Harry asked. "Can you fix it?"

"Not without some tools", replied Mark. "Come on - we've got a long walk back now."

Chapter 10

As they reached the clearing, carrying their helmets and the rucksack, Jess poked her head out of the tent. "What happened? Where's the quad bike?", she asked.

Mark explained that they'd got a puncture and he'd not taken the tool kit.

"Well, you won't do that again!", she said with a wry smile. "It's just over here – I'll get it for you."

"Thanks love", said Mark, as he took the plastic case. "Fancy coming back with me Harry?"

"Definitely!", replied Harry. "I can't wait to see how to fix a puncture."

"It probably won't be as dramatic as when we got the puncture", laughed Mark.

As they set off again, Harry slipped his hand into his dad's, turning to wave at Jess just before they rounded the trees at the edge of the clearing.

When they reached the stranded quad bike, Mark got to work. He started by placing a small jack underneath it to raise the deflated wheel off the ground. "Pass me the wrench, please", he asked Harry.

"Here you go", said Harry as he handed it over. He then watched his dad undo the wheel nuts before lifting the wheel off.

Mark placed the wheel on the ground and then used a tyre lever to remove the tyre. He felt carefully inside but couldn't find anything sticking through the tread.

"What caused it, Dad?", asked Harry.

"Hard to tell", replied Mark. "Could have been a sharp rock or a nail on the track perhaps." He showed Harry how to patch the tyre with a special tool to pull some tyre string through the hole to seal it. "Now for the hard part", he explained, pulling a foot pump out of his rucksack and attaching it to the tyre. They took turns on the foot pump and, after 5 minutes of effort, the tyre was hard once more.

"Yay!", shouted Harry, pulling on his helmet, "now we can get back."

Mark put the wheel back onto the quad bike and tightened the nuts, before lowering the jack and checking he had collected up all of the tools. Strapping the rucksack back onto the luggage rack, he gave Harry a thumbs up, before starting the engine and driving back to camp.

"So how are we going to build the cabin then?", asked Harry as they were finishing breakfast the next morning. "Do you have some plans to follow?"

"Sort of", replied Mark. "We've got some plans for the basic shape to make sure it's strong and won't fall down but then Mum and I thought we'd like to make some parts up ourselves so that it's individual to us." He took out a pen and some paper and sketched Harry a rough outline – "That's what we're aiming for", he said. "We're not actually building the cabin today though – we're preparing the site and cutting down some trees for the frame of it."

"Can I help?", Harry asked the inevitable question. "I'd really like to cut some trees down!"

"Hmmm", Mark said, "I'm not sure you're quite old enough to cut trees down but we'll be able to find you something to do, I'm sure."

Just then, there was the noise of an engine and Tim's pickup pulled up next to the tent. There was a large object in the back, covered up with a tarpaulin. "Morning folks", Tim said as he opened the pickup door.

"What's in the back, Tim?", asked Harry eagerly.

"Well, it's a plank saw – it lets you feed logs in and saws them into planks", Tim explained.

"We'll be using it to turn some of these trees into the sides and floor of the cabin", added Mark. The two men opened the tailgate of the pickup and heaved the machine out, followed by the generator which powered it.

As Tim drove off again, Mark explained what they would need to do that day. He was going into the village to pick up some more tools and equipment and Jess would start looking for suitable trees with Harry. "If you see anything really good, put an orange dot of paint on it so I can find it later", he suggested. There was also a flat pack tool storage shed which Tim had dropped off that they could build if they had time.

Jess and Harry picked up a notepad and pencil which Mark had sketched a rough layout of the clearing and surrounding forest in and a can of orange paint. Jess put them into a rucksack and they headed off to the far side of the clearing as Mark fuelled up the quad bike and set off into the village.

"Don't forget to go to the post office to see if the satellite phone has arrived!", shouted Harry as Mark rode off.

"I'm not sure he can hear you", laughed Jess, "but I'm sure he'll check – he's as keen to get it as you are!" Jess explained to Harry the kind of trees they were looking for and showed him with a tape measure how thick the trunks needed to be.

"How about this one, Mum?", he asked after a few minutes. "It looks nice and strong."

"I think that one is a little too tall", Jess replied, "we need to be able to cut it down safely, without it falling and hitting too many other trees."

After about an hour, they had identified 12 potential trees and marked them on the map and with orange paint on their trunks. "Time to go back and build that shed", suggested Jess.

"Ok, sounds fun", Harry agreed. He took his mum's hand as they walked back across the clearing to the tent. Once they had had a quick drink, Harry sliced the tape on the storage shed box and began to unpack the pieces. It looked like a giant Meccano set with metal panels, screws and nuts.

Jess picked up the instructions – "Ok Harry, let's lay out all of the pieces and work out what we start with", she proposed. It took a while to lay out all the components in order but it was then much easier to fit them all together and soon the outline of the shed was visible. The next job was to screw all of the metal side panels on – this turned out to be less fun than building the frame and Harry began to grumble.

"Oh Harry…", Jess said with a sigh, "things aren't always fun – sometimes we just have to do what we need to do first and then do the fun stuff later."

At that moment, Mark reappeared from his trip to the village. "Looking good, team", he said with a smile, giving Harry a thumbs up. "Guess what I got?", he asked, holding up a small brown box.

"The phone, the phone!", shouted Harry in excitement.

"I'll get it out later and we can work out how to use it", said Mark as he placed it inside the tent flap. "Now, how did you get on marking out trees?"

Jess showed Mark on the map where they had marked the trees and they went round to look at the orange dots so Mark could choose the best trees for himself. "I think we'll start with this one", he said, indicating a tall, sturdy tree on the other side of the clearing from the tent. "Harry, I want you to stay well back whilst I cut the tree – how about near the tent with Mum?"

"Ok Dad…", replied Harry – a bit miffed not to be in the thick of the action.

Mark put his hard hat, ear defenders and safety goggles on, along with some special armoured trousers and took the chainsaw across to the tree. He waved to

71

indicate that he was about to start cutting and then Harry watched as he cut a small notch on one side of the tree, before moving to the other side and making a deeper cut.

"He does that to make sure the tree falls where he wants it to", explained Jess. "The small cut is lower than the big cut so when the tree is almost cut through it starts to lean into the small cut and falls that way."

The chainsaw stopped and, for a moment, nothing happened, then there was a sharp crack and a swooshing noise as the large tree tumbled over and crashed to the ground. Harry started clapping and Mark took a pretend bow in his direction.

Next, Mark went along the tree trunk, slicing it into shorter pieces which would be light enough to allow him to drag them to the plank saw. He then came over and suggested Jess and Harry start digging out a trench around where the cabin was going to be built that they could sink the frame into. He had marked out the cabin layout with sticks pushed into the ground so that they knew where to dig.

"Are you tired, Harry?", Jess asked when he sat down for a rest after 5 minutes of digging. "It's quite warm out here for this kind of work." Mark came over and joined them, picking up Harry's discarded spade.

"We've got 3 trees down now, that's nearly enough for today", he explained. "I fancied a change for a few minutes and, since Harry's flagging, now seemed like the right time." He got to work quickly, helping Jess to make a deep foundation around the edge of the cabin site. "That's good", he said as he stepped back and admired their work, "once we've cut some of the wood, we can start to make the frame."

The trench dug, Mark went back to the treeline, aiming to cut one further tree down before starting to shape the trunks into planks. He started to saw but, as Harry watched, the tree began to lean to one side, then suddenly gave way and fell with an almighty crash right across the dirt track, blocking it completely!

What were they going to do now?

Chapter 11

"I'll make some lunch and then we can work out how to move the tree", suggested Jess. She disappeared into the tent to see what they had.

It was definitely time to try out the satellite phone now, thought Harry. "Dad", he called, "can I take the phone out of its box?"

"Yes", Mark smiled at him, "go ahead."

Harry rushed into the tent and emerged with the box in his hand. He sat down on the grass in front of the tent and carefully lifted up the flap on the top of the box. Inside was another box - this time with a picture of the phone printed on it. Harry opened the second box and slid out a plastic tray with the phone, a charging wire and an instruction booklet. "How does it work, Dad?", he called.

"Well you'd better pass me the instructions first", suggested Mark. "I've not used one of these before either." After a few moments reading and prodding at buttons, he let out a pleased sound. "Aha! So that's how you turn it on."

"Show me, show me!", said Harry, excitedly.

"It's not charged yet", explained Mark. "We need to set up the solar charger and leave it in the sun for a while first." He stood up and went over to the trailer where he rummaged around inside for a while before lifting out their solar charging pack. He carried it back over to Harry and sat it on the camp table. It was like a fat silver book which you opened out to reveal the solar panels inside. Mark plugged one end of the phone charging wire into the charging pack and the other into the phone. There was a quiet beep from the phone and a green light illuminated on the charging pack.

"Right", said Jess, emerging from inside the tent with some plates and a pile of cheese rolls. "We need to decide who is going to make the first call on this phone. I've got a challenge in mind." She had a shoe in one hand and a scarf in the other. "What we're going to do is take it in turns to wear this as a blindfold and then throw the shoe over our shoulder. Whoever lands closest to the chair I'm going to put in the middle of the clearing is the winner."

"Cool idea", said Harry. He was already jumping from one foot to the other in excitement.

"Do you want to go first, Harry?", she asked.

Harry nodded happily and Jess carefully wrapped the scarf around his head so that his eyes were covered, before picking up a chair and placing it about 20 metres away.

"Ready, Harry?" Jess checked.

"YES!", Harry shouted.

"Ok then – go!", Mark said as he and Jess stepped back in case they got hit by a wildly thrown shoe. Harry's throw sailed gracefully through the air and landed just behind the chair. Mark and Jess clapped loudly.

"How did I do?", asked Harry as he took off the scarf. "Oh wow! No-one's going to beat that!", he exclaimed.

Next up was Jess – Mark doing her blindfold and spinning her round twice to make it more difficult. Her throw was strong but totally in the wrong direction and landed closer to the track than the chair. Finally, Mark got his go. Jess span him round too and he twirled the shoe round in the air by its laces to show off before letting go. Harry held his breath – the shoe was headed right for the chair… He couldn't look and closed his eyes.

"Where did it land?", he asked when he opened them again.

"It carried on straight past and landed in a bush behind the chair", laughed Jess, "you won Harry!"

Harry was really excited but now he had to choose who to call – Karl or Bethany, or both? He soon discounted the last option as they wouldn't both be at the same house and Jess had said one call, not loads. He decided to wait and see how he felt when the phone was charged up.

As they ate their lunch, Mark was looking at the fallen tree – "We'd better get that tree moved once we've finished", he said.

"Why did it fall like that?", asked Harry.

"It just happens sometimes", replied Mark. "That's why I wanted you and Mum to stay well back. Our problem now is that we can't leave the track blocked and I was hoping to get some planks cut today still." Mark put down his plate, picked up his ear defenders and walked back over to the tree. He picked up the chainsaw and started to cut the trunk into more manageable pieces.

Once he had finished, Jess hooked a rope around the back of the quad bike and helped Mark to drag the pieces of tree away from the track.

"Can I help now?", asked Harry, "please."

"Ok", relented Jess, "hop on in front of me." She showed Harry how to operate the thumb throttle and then let him press it to move them forwards with her hand covering his in case of any slips.

"Wow, that was so exciting!", exclaimed Harry when they had finished. "I want to go on the quad bike again!"

"That was a special treat", cautioned Jess. "You're much too young to go on it by yourself, so I need you to promise that you'll leave it alone."

"Yes Mum", replied Harry. He'd really enjoyed the experience and was determined for them to let him go on it again soon.

"What's next, Dad?", Harry asked.

"Well, I think you've earned your phone call", Mark said. "I'll just check the phone and make sure it's got some charge in it." He came back and handed the phone to Harry. "Just got to decide who to call now", he said with a smile.

Harry looked at the phone and closed his eyes in concentration. Who to call – that was the question. Suddenly, it popped into his head – the school football team had been playing in the week and it was the first game since Harry had left. He had to call Karl and find out how they got on!

"Dad, have you got Karl's number please?", he said.

"Already programmed in for you", Mark answered. "I've put Bethany's in there too for when you want to call her."

"Thanks Dad", replied Harry. He scrolled down the list of phone numbers and stopped at Karl's. He pressed the green button and held the phone to his ear.

"Hello", came the eventual answer. The voice sounded very distant and slightly echoey.

"Hi, it's Harry, can I speak to Karl please?", Harry said quietly.

"Harry! Oh, how nice to hear from you", the voice said. Harry now recognised it as Karl's mum, though she still sounded like she was at the bottom of a hole. "I'll just get him for you. Are you having a lovely time?"

"Yes thanks, it's really fun", said Harry. The phone went quiet and there was a long pause before Karl came on the line.

"Harry! How are you?", Karl asked. "How's the woods and the tent and the animals and...."

Whilst Karl took a breath, Harry told him about their adventures at the riverbank and bird watching and how the tree this morning had fallen and blocked the road. "I almost forgot", he added, "how was the football match? Did you win?"

"Yes, we won", Karl said excitedly, "there was a new boy in the team and he was really good but I scored the winning goal!"

79

"Well done", congratulated Harry. He felt a little sad that he hadn't been there to play in the football match and that his friend was so far away but Karl's enthusiasm was making up for it.

"Bethany said to say hi to you if you called", Karl added. "We were hoping to hear from you soon. Did you get our letters?"

"Yes thanks", replied Harry, "they came a couple of days ago. I've written back but you probably haven't got it yet." He looked up to see both parents looking at him. "Um, I think it's time to go", he said, "I won the chance to use the phone first but now Dad wants to call Granny."

"Ok, mate. Thanks for calling – talk to you soon!", Karl replied.

"Bye Karl!", said Harry. He pressed the red button on the phone and passed it back to Mark.

"Cheer up Harry! We're calling Granny and Grandad now", smiled Jess, moving round to sit next to him. "It's nice to talk to people but we all feel a bit down afterwards."

Mark dialled a number on the phone and held it up to his ear. "Hi Mum", he said after a pause. Harry listened to his side of the conversation – Mark was explaining the same kind of things which he'd talked to

Karl about – what they'd been doing and some of the excitement that they'd had. After a few moments, he turned to Harry – "Would you like a word with Granny?", he asked. Harry held his hand out for the phone for the second time that afternoon.

"Hi Granny", he said into it. "How are you?"

"Hold on a minute dear, I'll put your grandad on", Granny explained. There was a pause and then Grandad spoke too.

"Hello Harry, how are you doing? Are you having fun?"

As Harry talked to his grandparents about riding on the back of the quad bike and how every meal felt like a picnic, he suddenly felt less sad about not being able to see them and more excited that he was able to share such fun experiences. Suddenly, there was a loud beep from the phone.

"Granny, Grandad, did you hear that beep?", he asked.

"I think the phone is running out of charge", Mark whispered to him.

"Sorry Granny, sorry Grandad, the phone battery is running out", Harry said. "I'll talk to you again soon..." With that, the phone suddenly went dead. Harry stared at it in surprise and then looked up to see his parents laughing.

"You didn't even get to say bye properly", chuckled Jess. "I bet they're looking at the phone at their end just as confused as you look, Harry!"

Chapter 12

It was morning and Harry was awake early. Mark and Jess had been up for ages already and the clearing was a hive of activity. Tim had been and dropped off ladders, a big workbench and various other tools and there was a constant growling from the plank saw as Mark cut more of the tree trunks down to size. Harry pulled a jumper over his pyjamas and went to investigate.

"Hi love", called Jess, seeing Harry emerge from the tent. "I'll get you some breakfast in a minute when I've finished helping Dad."

Harry nodded and walked over to the pile of tools to investigate. There was a big mallet, a large box of drill bits and a bright orange metal gun which looked quite like a water pistol.

"Be careful, Harry", shouted Mark, "that thing you're looking at is a nail gun and it's very dangerous."

"What's it for?", asked Harry.

"Well, it helps us to put the cabin walls up quickly by firing nails into the wood rather than hammering them", explained Mark. "They come out pretty fast though, which is why I really don't want you playing around with it."

"Ok", said Harry and wandered back to the tent to get dressed. When he came back out, Jess had poured him out a bowl of cereal and some juice.

"You'll need your strength today", she said, as she buttered some bread for him and put it on a plate. "Our job is to move a lot of the planks for Dad as he puts the cabin walls up."

After he had eaten, Harry helped Jess to pick up planks from the big pile by the storage shed and carry them over to where they had dug the trench a few days before. Mark had already got some of the larger logs down in the trench and was fixing them together. He explained that they fitted snugly by cutting notches out on each log and slotting the notches together. "It's a bit like they're holding hands", he said, showing Harry how one log sat with another.

"Is it going to be strong?", Harry asked. "I don't want it to fall down on top of me."

Mark laughed – "Don't worry Harry, this is the strongest and safest way to build a cabin. The notches stop the logs slipping and the weight of each one holds the others below down."

As Mark carried on dragging logs from the pile of trees he'd cut and notching them, Harry and Jess moved what felt like an endless pile of planks. "So, are these for the inside of the cabin?", asked Harry.

"Yes", replied Jess, "once the cabin outside walls are built, we'll nail these planks on the inside to give us a smooth wall. They will let us build some room dividers inside the cabin too."

"Is it going to be cold?", Harry asked. "It snows a lot in the winter here, doesn't it?"

"We're going to put in a log burner", replied Jess, "and Dad's arranged for some wool insulation to fit in the roof as that's where most of the heat would be lost."

They stepped back to look at progress – Mark had now got the cabin walls up to waist height and they had managed to move about half of the planks over to the building site.

"Where are the windows and doors?", Harry asked. "Has Dad forgotten them?"

"No", laughed Mark, who had overheard the question. "It's stronger if you build as if there are no doors and windows and then you cut them in later. It's ok, we won't have to climb in through the roof."

"Come on Harry", said Jess, "you can help me make lunch – I bet Dad's starving." They walked back to the tent where Harry spent most of his time watching

Mark's progress and didn't pay that much attention to the sandwiches he was helping to make. "Ham and jam, Harry? Are you sure?", she asked. "I think there was meant to be one ham sandwich and one jam one, not ham and jam together!"

As they took lunch over to Mark, Harry heard the sound of an engine approaching. It was Tim – he had come to help with the roof.

"Not quite ready for me yet, are you?", he joked. "I'll wait in the truck."

As Tim sat with them, eating the sandwiches he had brought, Mark explained how they were going to make the roof of the cabin. It was going to have some thick logs laid lengthways at the edges and the middle and then planks across them.

"It's a good job you brought those ladders earlier", said Mark. "I think we'll have to build up the walls at the ends of the cabin and then get the log for the middle of the roof up first. Once that's there, we can use a pulley to lift the other roof logs up."

"Good idea", replied Tim. "Those logs look pretty heavy."

"I've been lifting them all morning on my own!", grinned Mark.

As the friends got to work, Jess got out a drawing pad and showed Harry what she thought the inside of the cabin would look like. "Here's the main living area", she explained, showing Harry a space at the front of the cabin and about half the size. "We've got a little kitchen to the side, here, and then two bedrooms at the back."

"What about a bathroom?", asked Harry. "I don't want to use the shower on the side of the trailer all the time."

"We're going to make a bathroom outside initially", Jess said. "It'll be a separate little building with its own door. Dad needs to work out how we can store water to have proper taps and a proper shower and he doesn't want to build it as part of the cabin until he knows how he'll do it."

"That's ok", said Harry. "I was worried for a moment that we'd be showering outside when it was snowing!"

Jess laughed – "No danger of that, Harry. This is one lady who likes a warm shower, especially in the winter!"

As the day drew on, Harry and Jess watched Tim and Mark haul the big roof logs into place and then start nailing the planks covering the roof down. It was getting late and Harry's stomach was rumbling. As if he sensed it, Mark turned round and suggested they stopped for the day. "I'm knackered and I'm sure Tim is too", he said. "Let's have some tea and we can go again in the morning."

Tim said his goodbyes and drove off, leaving the three of them to admire the cabin's progress. Jess led Harry inside and showed him the space that her earlier drawing represented. She gathered some small tree branches and used them to mark out the different rooms. Harry was excited to see where his bedroom was going to be.

"It won't be big", Jess warned, "there's not loads of room in here and it'll be easier to keep warm if we're all quite close together. You'll have your own space though, which is the most important thing."

Harry didn't mind – this was all part of the big adventure and he was really looking forward to exchanging the tent for a more permanent home.

As Jess and Mark prepared the tea outside the tent, Harry lay on his sleeping bag writing a letter to Karl and Bethany. He told them about the cabin – explaining how it was constructed and drawing little pictures to show the different stages Mark had gone through during the day. When it came to explaining how the roof had gone on, Harry drew a picture of Tim and

Mark balancing on ladders, trying to winch a large log up on a pulley. He chuckled to himself – it had been really fun watching his new home being built and he hoped Karl and Bethany would be equally excited.

A few minutes later, Jess came in to tell Harry that his tea was ready and found him asleep on top of his sleeping bag, one hand clutching his pencil and the other 3 pages of neat handwriting. She gently shook his shoulder – "Tea's ready, Harry", she said. "You've had a really busy day but we've got lots to do tomorrow still. Come and eat something and we can tell you all about it."

Chapter 13

"Come on Harry", shouted Jess. "Dad's ready to go."
Mark was fastening his rucksack onto the luggage rack
of the quad bike and gave it a little tug to make sure it
was secure.

"Coming", replied Harry, as he ducked under the
tent flap and walked quickly over to his dad.

"Helmet?", asked Mark. "It's in the trailer."

Harry leaned inside the trailer, picked out his
helmet and put it on. "Bye Mum", he called as he
jumped on behind Mark. Jess waved as the quad bike
swung round in a big circle and headed down the track,
away from the clearing.

Harry held on around his dad's waist as they
bounced down the track. It was quite rough on the
stretch nearest the clearing but then got a bit
smoother further down, where there was more traffic
using it. They were headed to the post office and Harry
was hoping there would be a letter from Karl or
Bethany, or even both of them. It had only been a few
days since he wrote to them about the cabin build –
not enough time for them to have got the letter and
replied – but he was hoping they'd written anyway as
it would be a nice surprise.

Mark turned left instead of right at the bottom of the track and came to a standstill at the petrol station. "Just need to fill up", he said, "then we can head to the post office." He undid the petrol cap and filled the tank, before heading into the kiosk to pay. A couple of minutes later, he emerged with a packet of sweets in his hand and threw them through the air to Harry.

Harry caught the sweets – "Thanks Dad", he said before slipping them into his pocket. Mark jumped back onto the quad bike, started the engine and turned around to head up the road to the post office.

As they pulled up outside the post office and got off, Harry could see the big post truck disappearing down the road. He was suddenly excited – if the post had just been delivered to the post office then maybe there were letters for him inside. They entered the post office and Harry skipped over to the rack of postal boxes, tapping their one eagerly. Mark handed him the key and Harry opened the door. Nothing. His heart sank – he'd convinced himself that there would be something there for him.

Seeing the look of disappointment on his face, Mark put an arm round Harry's shoulders. "Don't be sad, Harry", he comforted, "Tim is popping by later – I'm sure he'll call in at the post office on the way to see if anything has come this afternoon." He then went on to explain that they had planned a hike for the rest of the day and would be trying to catch some fish from the river for tea. Harry cheered up and followed his dad back out onto the pavement.

They got back to the tent in double quick time – both looking forward to the hike and a chance to explore around the woods a bit more. Jess smiled when she saw them arrive – "I'm almost ready for the hike", she called. She was packing a rucksack with fishing equipment and snacks and had some rods in a long shoulder bag laying on the table next to her. Mark and Harry put their helmets back into the trailer, changed into walking boots and each picked up a bag.

Just as they were about to leave, Tim arrived with his pickup heavily laden. He jumped out and Mark went over to greet him.

"I thought you said Tim was coming later on?", said Harry.

"Well, I popped into the post office first thing and there was some mail for you", Tim told Harry. "I thought you might like it as soon as possible so I came early." He reached into the pickup cab and came out with two letters and a small parcel. Harry grabbed them eagerly.

"Thanks!", he said, grinning. The letters were from Bethany and Granny and the parcel was from Granny too. He shook it to his ear – "Chocolate", he guessed and then retreated to the tent happily to read his letters, the hike temporarily forgotten.

Mark helped Tim to unload – there were big solar panels, a wind turbine kit and some more ladders. Tim showed Jess the tall pole that the wind turbine sat on and could give them enough electricity for the cabin on days when it wasn't sunny enough for the solar panels.

Once Tim had left, Jess called to Harry – "Come on Harry, time for that hike!"

Harry led the way this time – they were following the same path down to the river as on their first trip and he remembered the way. He was excitedly pointing out the different trees that he'd learnt from listening to Jess on their various walks and the book that she'd given him to read. It didn't take long to reach the river and Harry was just about to rush to the bank when Mark stopped him.

"Woah, Harry, hold it there", he said. "Look over there, at the side of the river just near that tree."

In the shallow water, near the bank, was a tall grey bird with a long neck. Mark explained that it was a heron - "They eat small fish and other creatures in the

93

river." As Harry studied the heron, Mark went on to tell him that herons are particularly patient birds, often seeming to wait for hours for food to swim by.

"Wow", said Harry, "that is really cool!"

"Come on", Mark suggested, "let's head the other way to do our fishing, before he smells us." Mark told Harry that when they saw wildlife out in the woods it was best to keep a good distance so they didn't feel threatened. They backed away from the river bank and then, once in the trees, walked back the way they had come for a few minutes before turning to head back to the river further along the bank.

"This looks like a good spot", Jess said, dropping the bag she was carrying and stretching.

"Yes, this will do fine", agreed Mark. He opened the rod bag that he had carried and took out two fishing rods. They were in pieces and he screwed them together before attaching a reel and line.

"What are we using for bait?", asked Harry.

"Well, that's the clever bit", replied Mark. "We don't need any - salmon are often attracted by these colourful lures." He held out a feathery beaded hook – "Careful though, that's sharp", he warned.

Harry and Mark cast their lines into the river whilst Jess sat down with a book. "You boys can catch me my tea and I'll enjoy the sunshine", she said with a laugh. A few minutes passed by uneventfully and then Harry noticed his lure begin to wobble about.

"Dad, look!", he said, "it's wobbling about – that must be a fish."

"I think that's just the current", replied Mark. "Wind it in a bit if you like and see." Harry gently wound in the reel and felt it tugging back before the line suddenly went slack. "Well, whatever it was isn't there anymore", said Mark. Harry cast his line again, trying to get further this time and then settled down to wait.

Mark turned to talk to Jess about what they would be doing to the cabin next when she suddenly stopped and stared over his shoulder. "I think you've got a bite", she exclaimed. Mark looked back and saw his lure and the line moving frantically about in the water. He grabbed the rod and gently began to reel it in. Slowly, he moved the bucking line closer to the shore and eventually it broke the surface to reveal a large salmon. Jess grabbed a net and helped Mark land it.

"That's definitely big enough for our tea later", she said. "Lovely and fresh." Mark gutted the fish, throwing the waste parts back into the river for another creature to eat.

"I reckon a bird will spot those and have a tasty treat – maybe even that heron", he explained to Harry, who was wondering why his dad had apparently thrown rubbish into the river. "It's all part of nature – everything eats everything eventually."

They wrapped the fish up in a bag and slid it into the rucksack. "Can you take the rods apart, Harry?", asked Mark. He paused and thought for a moment - "Actually, why don't we make a campfire and cook our tea out here?"

They gathered some wood to make a small fire and Jess produced some potatoes she'd cooked earlier to have with their salmon. It was as if the campfire tea had been planned all along! As the fire crackled, Harry sat down with Mark to look at some animal books. Mark had been teaching him about the animals native to Canada and Harry was fascinated. His favourite so far was the moose but, apart from the first night experience, they had yet to see one.

Mark suddenly looked up, froze for a moment, and motioned to them to be quiet.

"Stay really still guys", he said. "Look over there, at the side of the river just near that tree."

Harry slowly turned to look and there, standing totally still, was a large brown bear. "What's it doing?", he whispered.

"It's fishing", replied Mark, "or rather it's waiting for fish to come by." He explained that bears caught fish by standing in shallow water and grabbing them in their claws when they swam by. As they watched, the bear suddenly swung out a large furry arm and emerged from the water with a silver fish in its paw.

As the bear ate the fish, it sniffed the air, then stopped and looked in their direction. It let out a low growl and started to walk purposefully towards them... "Aargh – is it going to eat us?!", cried Harry.

Chapter 14

"Back away really slowly", said Mark quietly. He stooped down and picked up their bags, leaving the fish on the ground. Jess took Harry's hand and they carefully walked backwards through the low bushes between the river bank and the woods beyond.

Mark didn't take his gaze off the bear, whilst trying to avoid direct eye contact. He quickly snuffed out the campfire and followed Jess and Harry away from the river. The bear carried on walking towards where they had been, sniffing as it went.

"I bet he can smell the salmon", said Mark in a low voice. The bear wasn't looking at them any more and they were almost at the edge of the trees. Once at the tree line, they retraced their steps through the wood. It was getting to be a familiar path now and soon they got a glimpse of the campsite and nearly completed cabin appearing through the trees. It was the first time Harry had seen the cabin from this viewpoint, and it looked really homely, even more so tonight.

"Phew", remarked Jess, "that was a bit close for comfort." She went into the tent and came out with a loaf of bread – "we'll just have to have a sandwich for tea now!"

Harry had been holding the reel of cable for what felt like ages, whilst Mark was at the top of a ladder, trying to fix one of the solar panels to the cabin roof. It was the morning and there was still some dew on the plank roof made from the trees Mark had felled. He had fixed a bracket across the roof to hold the top and bottom of the solar panels and was now trying to bolt them to it.

"Ok, Harry, can you pass me up that cable now please?", Mark asked. "I need to connect it to this panel and then run it down into the cabin."

As Harry passed the cable to his dad, he wondered how all of the panels would fit on the roof. "There's a lot of them", he said, "are they going on both sides of the roof?"

"Yes", replied Mark, "that way, we'll be able to use the sunshine in the morning and afternoon." He finished connecting the wire to the solar panel and passed it back down to Harry. "I've just got to fit another two panels on this side and then I can move round to the other side", he explained.

Harry watched him as he came down the ladder and then went back up, carrying one of the heavy panels.

He opened his notebook and started to draw a picture of his dad working.

"That's good, Harry – you should send it to Granny", Jess peered over his shoulder as she came to see how Mark was getting on. "I think she'd like to see what we've been up to, as well as reading our letters." Harry thought that was a good idea and reached for his colouring pencils to give the picture some added detail.

After a while, Mark was finished on the roof and moved inside the cabin to fit the lights and sockets. Harry followed him, interested in what was going on. "What's that?", he asked, pointing to a white box that Mark was fixing to the wall.

"It's called an inverter", Mark explained, "it turns the electricity from the solar panels into the kind of electricity that we can use." He pointed to a large box in the corner – "Those are batteries – the solar energy can be stored in there until we need it – so we can use things like the lights at night when there is no sunlight."

Mark stepped down from the step-ladder he had been using to fix the inverter and picked up some plug sockets – "These are normal plug sockets which I'm going to connect up and we can use to run appliances from."

"Can we use the computer once this is all finished?", asked Harry. He was very keen to be able to email Karl and Bethany so that he didn't have to wait for the post to arrive. It had been fun getting letters but sometimes he had written twice before he got a reply to the first letter and their news often seemed to cross over.

"Yes, we can", replied Mark. "Hopefully, we'll be able to set it up later today." He showed Harry a satellite dish that he'd already mounted on the cabin roof – "This will let us get the Internet so you can do your school classes", he explained. "There's no phone signal out here which is why we have the satellite phone and we had to find a similar solution for the Internet."

"That's really clever", said Harry, impressed. "We're in the middle of the forest and we can still get the Internet, just like at home."

"Did you want to give me a hand?", asked Jess. She had been stuffing moss that she had collected in a large bucket between the logs of the cabin walls. "This is to stop any draughts coming in during the winter so it stays nice and warm."

Harry picked up a handful of moss and Jess showed him how to roll it into a sausage shape and push it between two logs. It was fun and Harry had a little competition with Jess as to how long each could make their sausage. As they finished each area of wall, Jess carefully counted out how many planks they would need to cover it and make a flat surface. She piled the right number in front of the wall from the huge stack outside the cabin, ready for Mark to fix with the nail gun later.

"I've got something else to show you now", Jess told Harry when they had finished the end wall of the cabin. "We're going to make some light fittings so that we can use some of that electricity when Dad has finished."

"Can I help?", asked Harry. He liked making things and this sounded more fun than rolling sausages of moss.

"Of course you can", answered Jess. "Can you pick up those three glass jars by the door and bring them over here?" She showed Harry how to make a wall light by drilling a hole in the jar lid to attach a bulb holder, putting a bulb into it and then screwing the jar on to the lid. The bulb holders were angled and she then showed him how they would be screwed to the wall.

"How does the electricity get into them?", Harry asked, his head tipped to one side quizzically.

"Well, Dad is going to run some cables behind certain parts of the wall before he nails the planks on",

Jess explained. "That will let us connect up lights, switches and sockets."

Mark appeared at that point – "Wow, those look good, guys!", he exclaimed. "I guess you want me to finish the wall so that you can screw them on?"

"That would be nice", replied Jess, giving Harry a wink. "What have you been doing all this time?"

"Come and see", Mark invited.

They all stepped back into the cabin and Mark waved his arm at the maze of wiring, sockets and switches. "There you go", he said, "all we need for some comfortable living. I just need to nail the planks onto the wall and we're done with this job." With that, he picked up the nail gun and the first plank and set to work.

Later, after they'd had tea sitting in the sun outside the tent, Mark led them back over to the cabin. It was looking like much more of a home now. Outside was finished and, when they looked inside, it was a neat combination of planked walls and logs.

"Just got to put up some of the internal walls and then we can make some furniture", explained Mark. I'll do the walls in the morning and you can help Mum with the important things like beds", he suggested.

"Can we connect the computer to the Internet now?", asked Jess. "I could do with getting some ideas for curtains and things."

"Sure, let's give it a go", agreed Mark. He walked over to the trailer and returned with a couple of boxes and their laptop in its bag. He undid the first box and pulled out something small made of grey plastic. "This is the Internet router", he told Harry. "It takes the signal from the satellite dish and sends it to the computer." He plugged the router into one of the new sockets and then into the computer. "Just one more thing to do", he said, as he walked over to the fusebox and turned it on.

"That makes all the sockets work", Jess explained. "We're now using solar power!" She turned the computer on and, to their delight, the screen lit up and revealed all of the usual icons. Jess checked the lights on the router to make sure there was a signal from the Internet and clicked the browser button. The search screen launched and then suddenly everything turned off!

"What's gone wrong?!", cried Harry. He'd been looking forward to sending his first email.

"There's almost no power in the batteries", guessed Mark. "We only connected them up a little while ago and it hasn't been long enough to charge them." He looked at the computer and tried the power button again. Nothing. "I don't think the computer battery is charged either", he said. "We'll have to wait until the morning now – there's not a lot else we can do."

Harry thought about what had just happened. He wasn't sure whether to be happy or sad. He was looking forward to being more connected with his friends and being able to do some online schoolwork, but he'd also realised that once the computer was charged, his dad would have to start working properly. It had been loads of fun spending so much time together, exploring the forest and building the cabin but, once life returned to normal, would it start being just the same as at home but in a different place?

Sensing his mood, Jess put an arm around him. "Cheer up, Harry!", she said, "tomorrow we can sleep in the cabin for the first time." Harry smiled – now that WAS something to look forward to!

Chapter 15

The next morning, Harry was up early, eager to help get the cabin ready for them to sleep in. "What are we doing first?", he asked.

"Well, breakfast is probably a good place to start", smiled Jess. "I'm just making some porridge."

"Once we've eaten, we'll get our beds made", said Mark. "We need to have somewhere to sleep later and they're probably the most important piece of furniture."

Harry ate his porridge in double quick time. Jess had made some banana smoothies to have as well and he was slurping away at his when she slowed him down. "Steady on, Harry! You'll give yourself hiccups if you carry on like that."

After breakfast, they carried wood and tools over to the cabin and Mark explained how they were going to make the beds. "These long pieces will be the sides and we'll attach them to the thicker pieces over there which will be the legs", he said. He showed Harry a pile of smaller planks too – "These will be the slats across the bed."

"Isn't it going to be a bit hard to sleep on?", asked Harry.

"Well, we can use our airbeds from the tent to start with and later we'll collect some grass, dry it and stuff it in big sacks to make a mattress", Jess explained. "I've been getting all kinds of tips like that from the Internet before we came."

Harry held the lengths of wood together as Mark screwed them to make the bed frame. "Whose bed is this?", he asked.

"This is Mum's and mine", explained Mark. "Yours is a surprise so I'm going to be making that later while you give Mum a hand."

Harry was excited at the idea of a surprise. They'd been living so close together recently that he seemed to know everything that was happening before it actually happened, so something unexpected would be great.

Once the bed was made, Harry, Jess and Mark carried it into the corner which would become the main bedroom. "I'll put up the wall later", said Mark, "it's easier to do once the bed's in place as the rooms aren't going to be that big."

Mark then pulled out a notebook and showed Harry what else he was going to make – there were some cupboards, a table and a couple of benches. "The cupboards are for our bedrooms", he explained. "It will be nice to have somewhere to put a few things, even if the rest of the cabin is a bit chaotic." Harry didn't mind chaotic – it was starting to feel very homely in the cabin as more of the furniture was completed and he couldn't wait for the night to come so they could sleep there for the very first time.

"Do you want to help me next?", Jess asked Harry, as they finished off a cupboard together. "I'm going to make curtains for the windows." Mark had cut the window openings a few days earlier and fitted some simple frames with sheets of Perspex instead of glass. He had explained to Harry that it was recycled from someone Tim knew and would be a bit safer than glass.

Jess brought out some material from a bag which had been stored in the trailer and together they measured how wide the windows were. She then marked this out on the material, cut it to size and then folded the edges over. "This is called a hem", she explained. "We stitch along it to stop the edges of the material fraying." She showed Harry how to thread a needle with cotton and then stitch the edge of the curtain.

"This is quite tricky, isn't it?", he remarked a few moments later. "My stitches are all wobbly."

"Don't worry about that", laughed Jess, "the pattern in the material means you can't really see the stitches anyway!"

After a while, they had a passable pair of curtains for the front window and Jess called Mark over to show him. "They look great", he said, "I'm really excited to see what they look like on the window now." Jess caught his eye – she knew he was keen to keep Harry away from the bedroom furniture that he was building.

"Tell you what, Harry", she said, "let's see if we can find any spare wire in the trailer and then we can hang these up." They walked to the trailer together and managed to find enough wire for the window and also to hang a curtain over the door, in case of draughts. They went back to the cabin, screwed a couple of hooks either side of the window and attached the wire between them.

"How do we get the curtains on?", asked Harry.

"Silly me!", replied Jess. "I should have threaded the curtains onto the wire before we attached it to the hooks." She undid one end, slid the curtains over the wire and did it up again, before standing back to look. "Great, aren't they?", she said. "High five!"

Harry slapped the palm she offered and smiled. It was really nice making things with his mum and dad.

"Time for lunch", announced Jess. "Let's make some sandwiches, Harry." They walked back to the tent together and made a picnic to take back to Mark. There were cheese sandwiches, apples and some cake that Tim had brought them as a gift from his wife. Harry put in some of his chocolate from Granny too. "That's kind of you to share", Jess told him.

As they sat outside the cabin having their lunch, Harry asked what else they needed to do that day. "Well, I'm nearly there with your furniture now", Mark said, "then I'll put the walls up and we'll be sorted."

After lunch, Harry kicked a ball about with Jess for a while until Mark called them over. "Want to see your bedroom now?", he asked Harry. "You'll have to cover your eyes, so you don't spoil your surprise." Mark and Jess led Harry into the cabin and walked him to the corner. "You can open them now", said Mark.

Harry opened his eyes and in front of him was a cabin bed, up on high legs, with cupboards underneath and a little space for a den at one end. He started to say something, but no words would come out. Mark and Jess fell about laughing – "It's not often Harry is lost for words", Jess chuckled.

Eventually, Harry managed a response – "It's great Dad!", he cried, hugging Mark. It was going to be so much fun having a bedroom like this to play and snuggle down in. There was loads of room for his toys and the den space under the bed would be great for making his own hideout in. "Can we get our stuff now and move in?", he said, excitedly.

"Yes Harry, we can", replied Jess. "It's been a long wait but the cabin is ready now." They walked back to the tent together and Harry stuffed all his things back into the red bag. He picked up his sleeping bag and tucked it under his arm.

"Ready to go", he announced, and started to duck under the tent flap.

"Hold it Harry, give us a chance to catch up", said Mark, who was still looking for a bag to put some of his things in. After what seemed like ages, they walked happily back across to the cabin and Harry raced inside, threw his sleeping bag onto the bed and climbed on. He was home now and it really felt like it. All he had left to do was turn on the computer and dig out the instructions for emailing Karl and Bethany at long last. A few moments later, he'd composed an email to them both and his finger hovered over the SEND button. Harry thought about how much he had longed for this moment – to finally be connected back to his friends – it felt good. He pressed the button and imagined his email speeding across the sky, faster than any plane, taking his thoughts back home.

Later that evening, Tim came to see them with his wife Laura. She was amazed at the cabin and Harry spent at least half an hour walking her round inside and out, pointing out how they'd made different things. Tim and Laura stayed for tea – they'd brought steak as a new home present, so Mark got out the barbecue and soon there were delicious smells wafting across the clearing. As they ate, Tim and Mark talked about the work Mark would soon be doing and how the behaviour of the animals in the forest changed with the seasons. Laura told Jess about her job as a teacher and how some of the online lessons that Harry would be signing up for came from her school.

Harry sat back and looked at the cabin – the daylight was beginning to fade and Mark had turned the lights on inside. It looked really cosy and inviting and he couldn't wait to go to sleep in his new bed later. As a finishing touch, Mark had put a flagpole up outside the cabin and hung the Canada Wildlife Trust flag and Harry's old school football team flag on it. Harry smiled contentedly – it summed up the balance between their old and new lives in this lovely, remote part of Canada perfectly.

About The Author

Glen Blackwell lives in Suffolk, England. He has a career in finance and *We're Moving Where?!* is his first book. Inspired by bedtime reading with his 3 daughters, Glen loves to bring stories to life for young readers.

Glen would love to hear what you thought about *We're Moving Where?!* – please contact him as below:

www.glenblackwell.com

Facebook.com/glenblackwellauthor

Twitter: @gblackwellbooks

Alternatively, please leave a review on Amazon or your favourite online book store so that other readers can see what you thought.

Thank you!

Readers' Club

It would be great if you would like to join my Readers' Club. Sign up to receive a free eBook at **www.glenblackwell.com/readersclub**

You will also be the first to hear about Glen's new books and get the chance to become an advance reader for new titles.

If you are under 13 then please ask an adult to sign up for you.

Follow Glen

Facebook.com/glenblackwellauthor

Twitter: @gblackwellbooks

Printed in Great Britain
by Amazon